The Wonderful World of Disney

The
Ruby Bridges
Story

Adapted by **Hallie Marshall**

Teleplay by **Toni Ann Johnson**

Based on the life stories of
Ruby Bridges and Dr. Robert Coles

DISNEY PRESS

114 Fifth Avenue
New York, NY 10011-5690

Though the following novelization is inspired by actual events, the novelization is a dramatization that uses and adds fictional, composite, and representative characters and incidents for dramatic purposes.

Printed in the United States of America.

First Edition

1 3 5 7 9 10 8 6 4 2

This book is set in 12-point Berkeley Medium.

Library of Congress Catalog Card Number: 97-80134

ISBN: 0-7868-4210-5

Chapter 1

Brrriiing! A bell signaled three o'clock. At the Johnson Locket Public School the day was done. Though the building had been quiet just moments before, noise now grew inside the sand-colored walls, just behind the big double doors. Then the doors burst open and children streamed out—black children, brown, all children of color. And they were laughing, squealing, shouting out, running around. They were jumping and skipping. The sunlight was warm, and the children were happy to be free.

As they left the school building, Ruby Nelle Bridges leaned close to her friend Alison Lewis. She was talking to Alison about something, maybe something secret, or maybe telling some kind of joke. Ruby's little sister, Mary, struggled to catch up. But Mary didn't hear what they said. Ruby and Alison were already giggling, best friends, both six years old, first graders, thick as thieves.

On such a good, sweet-smelling afternoon, even a tiny neighborhood softball game could attract an audience. People surrounded the grassy lot on Logan Street, watching and sometimes cheering. There were grown-ups and kids, mothers and fathers, grandparents, babies, neighbors.

Ruby scuffed the dirt and eyed the batter. She was playing third base, and there were runners aboard. Alison for one. Alison was on the other team, waiting on second, ready to go. Then *crack*! Alison streaked to third. Safe there, she stuck out her tongue at Ruby.

Ruby shrugged. She didn't care. At least she pretended she didn't care. Her friend settled in with her foot on the base and looked around at the crowd. "Ruby Nelle," Alison asked, "where's your mama at?"

"Shhhh," said Ruby. The game was close and she didn't want to be distracted. She gave the next batter her attention. "Mama's got company."

Ruby's mother was just sitting down at the kitchen table. Across from her, Dr. A. C. Broyard tucked his fork neatly into a piece of cake. "Oh, my," he said. "Lucielle, this is wonderful."

"It's from scratch," Ruby's mother told him. Lucielle was a good cook and proud of the fact. And the doctor was an important guest.

"You have a gift indeed," he said. "And speaking of gifts, let me explain why I'm here." Dr. Broyard put down his fork and touched his mouth with a napkin. "Your Ruby scored very well on the school-board exam. Very, very well. In fact, Ruby did better than most of the first graders in the entire district."

Lucielle smiled at him. She knew her girl was smart. Dr. Broyard returned the smile and picked up his fork again.

Poised over home plate, Ruby held the bat tightly. The pitch came in. Ruby swung hard. She sent the ball sailing high and far, way out into the street. Then she ran. As she rounded first base, then second, she could hear cheering. And she could see that someone had retrieved the ball. They were after her. Ruby ran to third.

Someone was shouting: "Go on, baby girl!" Ruby knew it was her father. Ahead was a blur that was Alison, the catcher, crouched at home plate. Ruby squeezed her eyes shut and ran.

"Safe!" Ruby's daddy yelled.

"Out!" That was Mr. Lewis, Alison's dad.

But the crowd sided with Ruby's father. "Home run!" they yelled. "She was safe! Safe! The girl was safe!" And Mr. Lewis finally had to agree.

Chapter 2

The softball game was over. Ruby's dad held out his arms and scooped up his oldest girl. He was wearing his uniform from the garage where he worked. His clothes smelled of cars and engine oil. Ruby grinned at him, then snuggled into his embrace. Something somewhere made a crackling sound. "What's that?" she asked.

From his pocket, Abon drew out a small waxed-paper bag. He held it briefly under Ruby's nose. Doughnuts! "We're gonna get us some milk," he told her.

Abon put his daughter down and took her by the hand. As they walked the street together, past the corner bar and toward Stein's, Ruby and her dad waved at people they knew. Most were black, though some were white. Everyone waved back.

Stein's grocery store was painted cleanly and had a big front porch. Mrs. Stein always looked soft, as if someone had dusted her with powder. Ruby liked her. While her father got the milk, Ruby reached way up to put a few coins on the counter.

"Why, Ruby Nelle," Mrs. Stein declared, "it looks like you've been growing. Seems just last week you couldn't see over the counter."

Ruby giggled. She was standing on her tiptoes.

"And a roll of bologna, too," her father said. "Please, Mrs. Stein."

Mrs. Stein was surprised. "Lucielle just bought a roll two days ago."

Abon sighed. "Five kids, ma'am. And they can eat like an army platoon!"

As Ruby and her father went up the walkway to their house, their company was just leaving. Abon shifted the grocery sack over and held out his hand. Dr. Broyard shook it.

"Dr. A. C. Broyard of the NAACP," he introduced himself. "Glad to meet you, Mr. Bridges."

The NAACP. Ruby knew what those letters meant. They stood for something important she had learned by heart. Dr. Broyard was with the National Association for the Advancement of Colored People.

He looked down at Ruby and smiled. "Is this the little girl I hear is so smart?"

Ruby guessed so. She nodded and smiled shyly back.

Dr. Broyard bent toward her. "Congratulations, honey," he said. "You've been picked with five other special girls. And you're about to do something no other Negro children have done in New Orleans."

Dr. Broyard straightened and tipped his hat to her father. "You've got a lot to be proud of," he said.

Ruby looked from one face to the other. What was going on?

There were five kids in the Bridges family: first Ruby, and then her sister, Mary, then Carl; Alton was just a toddler, and there was the baby, Wayne. When they played together, they could jump and bump and make some noise. But at bedtime Lucielle wanted quiet.

"Hey," said their mother. She stood in the doorway. "On your knees!"

The children quieted right away. They knelt by the bed to pray. "Now I lay me down to sleep. . . ." Even the toddler knew a few of the words.

As Lucielle tucked them in, Ruby remembered something. "Mama?"

"Shhhh." Ruby's mother kissed her. She put her cheek against that of her daughter. Downstairs, Lucielle could hear the sounds of the TV news. "Go to sleep, baby," she said.

"But, Mama," Ruby asked, "what's it mean I've been picked with five others?"

Chapter 3

"In Baton Rouge today, Governor James Houston Davis called for a special legislative session to determine how to stop the impending racial mixing in the New Orleans public schools. The Attorney General of the United States warned the governor not to interfere with the federal court order to desegregate the schools. Governor Davis, however, vowed to preserve segregation despite the warning. . . ."

Abon watched the reporter closely. In 1960, in New Orleans, white children went to school separately from others. "Separate but equal," or so it was said. Things had been that way for a long time, and change was slow in coming. Anything that brought on change also brought on heated words *and* trouble.

So Abon listened, and what he was hearing worried him. When the television news flashed to something else, he switched off the set. "Cielle," he said. "We've got to talk about this."

"I heard," she said. "And I'm not letting it scare me. Governor Davis can fuss all he wants, but the federal government is above the state, so he ain't got no choice."

"But why do we gotta put Ruby where she ain't even wanted?" Abon pointed to the silent TV. "If she did so

7

good on that test, that must mean she's doing just fine where she's at."

"Abon, you know the colored schools aren't as good as the white ones." Lucille's voice was determined. "And Dr. Broyard says that Ruby has what it takes to really go far. Nobody ever took that kind of interest in me or you as kids, did they? If Ruby does this, it could make things better for our other kids, too. For all colored kids!"

Abon shook his head. No, nobody had. He thought it over as Lucielle went on. "Ruby won this right with her own mind. So don't you think she deserves to take it?"

She waited there for an answer, and Abon didn't have one. He'd seen trouble coming on before, and he was seeing it now.

At church on Sunday the message was all about skin color and fire. The pastor told his congregation it was time for America's darker brothers and sisters to rise up. He said that people of color needed to rise up and walk through the fire.

As the choir sang "You'll Never Walk Alone," Abon and his family sang along. But Abon's eyes still held the worry of the night before. He looked at Ruby singing there, and he thought of her walking through fire. She was small, and she was his daughter, and he loved her very much.

So after church, after the sermon and the singing and the prayers, Abon and Lucielle talked it over, keeping the preacher's sermon in mind.

8

Ruby walked home from church with Alison. She barely paid attention to Carl or Mary alongside her, or to Alison's parents. Ruby had something on her mind.

"So you ain't gonna be walking with us tomorrow?" Alison asked.

"I'm going to the new school," Ruby told her. "We get to ride in a car. That's what Mama says."

Alison looked sad, and Ruby wanted to cheer her up. As they rounded the corner onto Logan Street, she said, "I'm still gonna see you after school. And I'm still gonna whup your butt in softball."

"Nuh-uh," Alison said. "You can't whup me!" She laughed, thinking of the close call of the last game. "Ruby Nelle Bridges, you know you was out!"

Chapter 4

The next morning, Ruby sat at the kitchen table with her father. His uniform was clean and smelled only of soap. "You nervous, baby girl?" he asked her.

Ruby looked at him and considered whether she felt nervous. "Kind of," she said.

"It's gonna be fine. I promise." And he hoped that was true. Abon stood and leaned down to kiss Ruby on the forehead. "Wish I could go with you, baby," he said. "But you can tell daddy all about it later, okay?"

Ruby hugged him. She hugged him hard.

There were guards and barricades lining Logan Street. The guards stopped Abon as he was on his way to work, carrying his lunch bag. "Are you a resident here?" one of them asked.

Abon was uneasy. "Yes," he said, very simply.

"Do you have identification?" The guard who asked seemed friendly, as though he were just doing his job.

Abon reached into his pocket, but the guard waved him on. He wouldn't need identification to leave, but he would need it to return home. That didn't feel right. As Ruby's father walked past the barricade, the troubles returned to his thoughts.

Back in the kitchen, Mary was being insistent. "Do mine, too, Mrs. Taylor!" she begged, but Mrs. Taylor was busy combing out Ruby's hair.

Lucielle looked up from feeding the baby. "Mary," she said, "this is Ruby's day." There wasn't much time before school, and she wanted Ruby to look especially nice on her first day there.

"Now, Ruby," her mother reminded her, "call the teacher 'ma'am' when she speaks to you. Okay, baby?"

"Yes, Mama," Ruby said. She twisted around to ask Mrs. Taylor a question. "Do you think those other girls who got picked will sit with me at lunchtime?"

Outside the house, two sedans drew up to the curb. Some very tall men got out of the second car. The men wore armbands that read DEPUTY U.S. MARSHAL around the sleeves of their suits.

The tall men waited as the door opened. Lucielle and Ruby stepped out hand in hand. Lucielle looked from one man to the next, then back to her children in the doorway. "You all mind Mrs. Taylor," she said. "You hear?"

With that taken care of, Ruby's mother squared her shoulders. "I thought the man from the NAACP was—"

"You're being escorted by U.S. marshals today, ma'am," one of the men explained.

The other marshal smiled in a friendly way. "Good morning," he said.

Lucielle answered quietly. "Morning," she said. She held onto Ruby's hand as they got in the car.

From the sidewalks, from the windows of houses, from the porches around them, the neighborhood was watching as the two sedans proceeded down Logan Street. One car drove in front of the car with Ruby and her mother. They were waved past the barricades, onto another street, and another, then around a corner.

Just ahead, Ruby could see the red brick walls of her new school, the William Frantz Public School. There were many bodies, like a parade—mostly white people, mostly women. The people looked angry.

From her seat in the car Ruby cried, "Look Mom, it's Mardi Gras!"

From the seat in front, one of the marshals turned around. He spoke to Ruby and her mother. "Wait until I open the door before you get out. We'll be behind you," he said. "The men in the other car will walk in front of you."

Lucielle held Ruby close and nodded.

"Stay between the four of us, and do not look back," the marshal went on. "No matter what happens, don't look back at the crowd."

Chapter 5

Dr. Robert Coles was annoyed. With an impatient gesture, he turned back the cuff on his air force uniform. The watch on his wrist said he was late. He honked the horn of his Ford car, then rolled down the window to see what was happening.

"No sense making noise," a policeman told him. "Ain't nothing going through."

"I'm trying to get to a medical conference," Coles said. "What's going on here?"

The officer nodded toward the two sedans ahead. As the doors of the first car opened, two tall men got out. Two more men got out of the second vehicle. One of them opened the door for Ruby and Lucielle.

With her head held high, Lucielle took the small hand of her daughter. Two of the men moved in front of them, and two moved in behind. They were surrounded.

From the crowd came voices that said terrible things, and the shouting grew into a chant: "Two, four, six, eight! We don't wanna integrate! Two, four, six . . ."

Holding her mother's hand, Ruby approached the stairs to her new school. She stared straight ahead.

"Two, four, six, eight! We don't wanna integrate!"

The noise swelled around Ruby. The stairs were steep, and she climbed them. She didn't look back.

Stuck in the crowd but not of them, Bob Coles could only watch.

Inside the building, doors opened and closed as teachers came out to see what the fuss was about. Some kids poked their heads into the hallway. "Get back!" one of the teachers told them.

The marshals escorted Ruby and her mother to the school's administrative office. The office had a big glass window that looked into the hallway, so the administrative vice principal could keep an eye on things. Her name was Miss Woodmere.

Ruby whispered a question to her mother. "Mama, where's the other girls?"

"What about the other children?" Lucielle asked. "They told me there were two more supposed to be coming here with Ruby."

"I suppose," Miss Woodmere said, "their parents had the good sense not to put their children through this."

They what? Ruby wondered. Through the window she could see parents dragging their children through the hallways, taking them from the classrooms and out of the school, saying things like, "It ain't gonna happen!" One mother screamed, "My kid ain't goin' to school with *their* kind!"

Miss Woodmere turned to look through the window,

too. Her face was blank, without feeling. When a police officer knocked at the door, Miss Woodmere went slowly to answer.

"Miss Woodmere," the policeman said, "there's a woman who says she's a new teacher. She don't look like no teacher, though. You know anything about it?"

The woman was Mrs. Barbara Henry. She was young and stylish. Miss Woodmere looked her over and said sternly, "You don't look like a teacher. The police must have thought you were a reporter."

Barbara didn't know how to reply. "Good morning," she said at last. She held out her hand. "Superintendent Redmond told me to report to the principal for work today."

"Not today," Miss Woodmere told her. "The principal is downtown at a school board meeting today. It's not sorted out just yet."

The clock on the wall said eleven o'clock . . . eleven thirty . . . twelve. Lucielle and Ruby ate their lunches. No one came to speak with them. They waited through the afternoon. Ruby couldn't keep her eyes open. She leaned up against her mother and fell asleep.

At three o'clock Miss Woodmere dismissed them. Lucielle was angry and looked the vice principal right in the eye. Miss Woodmere, not expecting this reaction, was a bit flustered and walked away. Lucielle nudged Ruby. Ruby awoke with a start. "This school's easy!" she said. She smiled at her mother.

Chapter 6

That evening, Ruby sat on the porch with Alison. They could see the guarded barricades further on down the street. Lights and the sound of distant voices intruded on the peaceful night. The girls were eating freeze pops, and they were talking seriously.

Alison asked, "You like riding in that car with those white men?" To her surprise, Ruby nodded. "My daddy says I gotta go to Catholic school starting soon," Alison told her friend, "and we ain't even Catholic."

Ruby sucked on her freeze pop and thought about it. "Why?"

"Catholic school is private," Alison said with some importance, "and Daddy says he wants me to be with better kids."

"What's better about 'em?" Ruby asked. But Alison shrugged. She didn't know.

Over in a different neighborhood, on a street that had no guards or barricades, Dr. Coles and his wife, Jane, were sitting down to dinner. The television was tuned to the news, but Bob Coles was talking over it.

"It was incredible!" he told his wife. "People were

chanting, yelling hateful things at this little tiny girl. You would have died."

"No," said Jane. "I would have gotten in a fight with them."

Coles was excited. "If I could work with this girl . . . if I could see how she copes with the stress, it would be a great addition to my work with other kids."

He looked over to see if Jane understood. She smiled at him. "I've got to go back there," he continued. "I've got to find a way to meet her."

Behind him, the television screen flickered with scenes of rioting and protest. Bob Coles wasn't paying attention. But back in their house on Logan Street, Lucielle and Abon were.

"Angry youths continue to surge through the streets of New Orleans tonight in demonstrations against forced integration at the William Frantz and McDonogh Schools. . . ."

Abon couldn't believe what he was seeing. "They're acting crazy," he said. "This ain't safe, Lucielle." He looked over at his wife.

Lucielle's eyes held pain and something else, something strong. "Ruby will be fine," she said. "She's got God and the government protecting her. And those crazy fools are gonna find out it's not easy to make us quit."

Chapter 7

The next morning there were more people outside the school than the day before. The crowd had grown overnight, and the noise had grown along with it. There were hundreds of people: men, women, and children. They carried signs that said WHITES ONLY! And someone had painted a message across the entryway: NO NIGGERS!

Dr. Coles stood within the crowd. Like them, he was waiting for Ruby, though he didn't share their anger.

Inside the school building, Miss Woodmere was taking charge. As she showed Barbara Henry around, it was clear the vice principal didn't like her newest teacher. "I don't envy you," Miss Woodmere said. "You must have really needed a job."

The sounds from outside filtered into the hallway. A chant was working up from the crowd: "Two, four, six, eight! We don't wanna integrate!"

Barbara Henry listened for a moment, then she looked Miss Woodmere straight in the eye. "I've taught many kinds of children," she said, "and I enjoy them all."

When the car with Ruby and her mother came around the

corner, the noise grew louder and the people pressed frighteningly close. In the front seat, the marshals felt for their guns. In the back, Lucielle held Ruby tight. "Don't look back," one marshal said. "Remember what I told you."

As on the day before, Bob Coles watched the men in the two sedans get out. He saw them open the rear door of the second car. Once again, the men surrounded Ruby and her mother.

In spite of the ugly words that swirled around them, in spite of the chant and the hate and the spittle—in spite of it all, Lucielle and Ruby walked hand in hand up the stairs and into the red brick school.

Things inside were calmer, quieter, but in a very strange way. There were teachers there, and police officers, the principal, and a few other grown-ups. But there were no other children. None. Ruby was the only one who had come to school.

Barbara Henry met her just inside the entrance. "Hi, Ruby Nelle," she said. "I'm Mrs. Henry. I'll be your teacher." She smiled at Ruby and then at Lucielle. "It's nice to meet you, Mrs. Bridges."

Ruby's mother let out a breath. Unconsciously, she'd been holding it. At least something had changed from the day before. "Likewise," she said.

Ruby's new teacher led her to a room down the hall. Lucielle followed, as did the U.S. marshals. The men took up positions on either side of the door. They were guarding the classroom.

Barbara Henry was a little nervous. The protesters, while still present, had simmered down. "There was a phonics book here a moment ago," she said. "Let me see if I can find it."

As Barbara searched for the book, the crowd could be heard through the open windows. "Keep this a white school!" somebody shouted. "Go home!" Then there was the chant: "Two, four, six, eight . . ."

"I haven't quite gotten my bearings," Barbara apologized. She tried to ignore the noise outside. "That book should be right here. . . ."

All at once, the teacher stopped pretending. She went to the windows and closed them. Lucielle helped. "Where are you from?" Lucielle asked.

"I'm from Boston," Barbara said. "But I've been teaching overseas." The teacher fanned herself. It was hot with the windows shut. "Goodness," she said, "the humidity here is really something!"

"Welcome to the South," Lucielle told her.

Chapter 8

While the new teacher got her bearings and put her student to work, Bob Coles was ushered into the office. Coles was handsome, and Miss Woodmere was inclined to be pleasant. "And what can I do for you?" she asked.

"I'm a psychiatrist," he said. "I've come because I'd like to talk with the Negro child. . . ."

Miss Woodmere's face took on a frown. "What would you wanna talk to that little nigra for?"

"I'd like to see how she's doing," Coles said quickly. When Miss Woodmere didn't respond, he got professional and stuffy. "The focus of the work I'm pursuing involves studying how children handle stress. The way children cope with crises intrigues me."

"I can tell you right now," Miss Woodmere announced, "there's nothing 'intriguing' about that colored girl—"

Bob Coles interrupted her. "I respect your opinion," he said, though he thought otherwise. "I'd like to speak with her mother. I'd like to know the child's name."

The principal shook her head. "I can't help you," she told him. "I can't get any more involved than I'm required to. I'd be breaking the law. You ought to go talk to their organization."

"What organization?" he asked.

"That *colored people's* organization." She seemed annoyed.

In the classroom Ruby was working hard. She liked her teacher. Mrs. Henry thought of interesting things to do. When the bell rang for lunchtime, Ruby was almost disappointed.

"I'll be back in half an hour," the teacher promised.

Ruby's mother had been watching them together. She was thinking that she liked Barbara Henry, too. "We'll eat right here," Lucielle said. She brought out a thermos and some sandwiches.

Barbara stopped a teacher whose name was Jill as she was walking down the hallway. The teacher showed the way to the lounge, but she wasn't very friendly. And when Barbara came into the room she was greeted with stony silence.

Finally the others began to talk, and they talked as if Barbara weren't there. "Well," said one, "so long as I get paid, this place could burn down for all I care."

"Oh, please," another teacher broke in, "a few more days of doing nothing, and you'll be itching to get busy."

Barbara couldn't help it. "It seems silly," she said, "for the whole school to empty out over one little child." She smoothed her skirt and sat down. "I should hope they're handling things better at the McDonogh School."

The first teacher decided it was time to set Barbara straight. "My friend gave her resignation so she wouldn't have to teach that nigra! Nothin' silly about it! I don't know where you're from, but 'round here we may not be fancy but we don't teach nigras, and our kids don't *learn* with them!"

The silence settled once again. Without hunger, but with great deliberation, Barbara got through her lunch.

Lucielle put the cap back on the thermos. "Ruby Nelle?" she said. Ruby was engrossed in a book, "I know this word, and this word, and *this* word, Mama!" As Ruby pointed out the words to her mother, Lucielle had to ask. "How are you doing?"

"Fine," said Ruby. "I can *read*, Mama."

"That's good, baby." Ruby's mother smiled at her. "But remember I've got to go on back to work tomorrow." Lucielle worked as a maid.

"Can you be brave and come to school with the big men by yourself?"

Ruby considered the question so seriously that Lucielle's eyes brimmed with tears. At last her daughter nodded. "Okay," she said.

"That's my brave girl," Ruby's mother said. She wanted to be braver herself, and to quit crying. "Finish your sandwich," she ordered.

"Mama?" Ruby asked. "Where are all the other kids?"

Her mother picked up the sandwich crust and put it in the lunch bag. "They're . . . out for now," she answered. "They'll be back soon."

"When?" Ruby wanted to know.

Lucielle pointed to Ruby's cup. "Finish your milk," she said.

Chapter 9

At home that evening, there wasn't much playing or jumping around. When their mother came to tuck them in, the children had already said their prayers. Lucielle kissed Mary good night, then Carl. When she bent down to kiss Ruby, she whispered, "You know, Jesus faced a mob, too, baby. Just like you."

Ruby listened as her mother went on. "And do you know what Jesus did? He prayed for those people, because they didn't any know better. Jesus was trying to teach them something. He prayed for them to understand."

Lucielle gave her daughter another kiss. She switched off the light and went downstairs. Abon was reading the paper.

"This is dangerous, Cielle," he told her. "It's only day two, and I've already had enough."

Abon wanted to quit! Lucielle couldn't believe it. "Why are you always so scared of everything?" she asked him. "You're never gonna have nothing if you're too afraid to take it!"

Abon slapped the paper shut. "I fought in the Korean War," he said. "I won a Purple Heart. You think I got that medal being scared?"

Lucielle softened. "No," she said. "I'm sorry." She tried to explain, "It's just that Ruby earned the right to better schooling. That school is bigger, it's newer, it's cleaner. That school is better."

"Ruby's supposed to go there alone tomorrow." Abon's voice broke with the thought. "She's gonna go alone. How can we put her through that?"

Lucielle remembered. The idea of Ruby walking through the crowd by herself made her want to cry. But she was determined. "Abon," she said. "I'm tired of people telling us where we can't go, what we can't do, what we ain't supposed to have. That's the way we were raised."

When her husband didn't answer, Lucielle continued softly on. "Our children deserve better," she said. "And the only way things are gonna get better is if we make them better. We can't be scared away from that."

Abon stared down at the newspaper. He wasn't afraid for himself. He was afraid for Ruby. "She's our baby, Lucielle. And I don't want nothing bad to happen to her. She's just a little girl."

Chapter 10

On the third day the mob had grown larger, louder, and more frightening. The crowd was fueled by heated words and hatred. Standing within it, Bob Coles felt very uncomfortable. He took out a small notebook and a pen, as if those things could soothe him. He told himself he was a doctor, present only to observe.

Once again, he watched the sedans pull in front of the school. He heard the noise from the people. But when the marshals opened the door of the second car, Ruby stepped out alone.

They shouted at Ruby, they screamed out terrible things. They called her a nigger. They said they'd kill her. The men flanked Ruby and kept going. She had a little bow in her hair, a white bow, that bounced along as she walked.

A strong, stocky woman pushed in front of Coles. She yelled at Ruby. "I'm gonna poison you! I'm gonna poison you 'til you choke to death!"

Ruby heard the woman's threat. Her eyes grew wide. "Don't look, Ruby!" one of the marshals told her.

Ruby didn't look. She didn't turn back. Bob Coles caught a glimpse of the white bow as Ruby walked into her school.

Barbara Henry met her at the entrance. She took Ruby's hand and walked her down the hall. The other teachers, including Jill, the teacher who had directed her to the lunchroom, stood in a cluster and watched them walk by. Not one of them smiled or said a word. To distract Ruby, Barbara said, "You look so cute today! That dress is lovely, and your bow matches it so well."

Ruby smiled at Mrs. Henry, feeling flattered and accepted.

Jill looked down at the ground. She was ashamed of herself.

The day went by fine until lunchtime. Ruby wasn't hungry. She sat alone in the classroom and waited for Barbara Henry to return. And when she did, Ruby set herself to learning more. Her teacher could hardly keep up.

So after school was over, Barbara Henry went to talk with Miss Woodmere. Miss Woodmere had her handbag out. She was buttoning a sweater. She was ready to go. "What is it?" she asked coldly.

"I just wanted to speak with you about my student," Barbara replied. Miss Woodmere walked down the hall, and Barbara tagged behind her. "Ruby has no physical education. She can't go play at recess. She should have some type of music lesson. There are lots of things . . ."

Miss Woodmere only walked faster. "Due to your student," she hissed, "I don't even have time to think! As you well know, we're supposed to leave the school grounds right away. We're not allowed to stay here."

Barbara trotted after her. "That's not due to my student!" Barbara was almost shouting. "That's because of people's attitudes toward my student! And that's not any fault of Ruby's!"

After school Ruby and Alison played jacks on Alison's front porch. Ruby had just gotten to the threes. She bounced the ball. "So," she asked her friend, "you Catholic yet?"

"Nuh-uh." Alison shook her head. "Those nuns are too mean! They hit me on my knuckles!"

"Mean?" Ruby was shocked. "*My* teacher is nice."

Ruby missed, and Alison took her turn. "Daddy says that sore knuckles are the price you pay for going to private school. And private school is better."

Ruby looked thoughtful. "You got lots of kids in your class?" When Alison nodded, Ruby said, "It's not private then. My school is private. I'm the only one there!"

Alison didn't like being one-upped. "Daddy says those guards and barricades on our street are there because of you, because you wanted to go to that school. My daddy says it's *your* fault."

Chapter 11

Ruby's father wasn't eating his dinner. He sat and looked at the food on his plate. On the kitchen counter were two huge bags of doughnuts. Ruby could see them. "Daddy?" she asked. "Ain't you hungry?"

"Guess not," her father answered.

"I'll eat it," Carl chimed in. "I want to."

Abon passed his plate over to Carl. "You're gonna eat us into the poorhouse," he said.

"Why'd you bring so many doughnuts?" Ruby wanted to know. But her father didn't reply. He just stared at the empty spot where his plate had been. When Lucielle prodded him, Abon forced a smile and said, "I'll tell you why I got so many doughnuts. Folks down at the bakery heard what a brave thing you was doin' and they wanted to give you and your brothers and sister an extra-special treat."

That night Abon didn't turn on the television. He didn't read the paper. When Lucielle came downstairs, he was washing dishes. "The kids are asleep," she told him. She picked up a towel and began to dry. "You want to tell me what's going on?"

Her husband rinsed a plate. "The boss told me

today . . . he said he couldn't have a nigger working for him that's got a child in a white school.'"

Lucielle put the towel down. Worry pushed at her. "I've been working there four years," Abon went on. "Never had one unhappy customer. Not one. Nobody's better at fixing cars than me."

His wife put a hand on his arm. "We'll work it out," she said.

Abon glanced over at the doughnuts on the counter. "The man who owns the bakeshop felt sorry for me, I guess. He gave me all the doughnuts he had. And when I said I didn't want them all, he told me not to worry. He said he could always make more."

Abon was upset. "What can *I* make more of, Lucielle?" He turned and walked out of the room.

Lucielle followed. "Abon, don't—"

He interrupted her. "I was in the army," he said. "I know about integration. They didn't treat me the same as any white soldier. I was a *colored* soldier! Second-class!"

Abon's voice had gotten louder. "Shhhh," said Lucielle. "The Lord's gonna make a way for us," she told him uneasily.

Abon looked over at the picture of Jesus that was hanging on the wall. Jesus was white in the picture. It didn't give Abon any comfort.

The next day, the NAACP took a hand in things. Dr. Broyard and his wife came to Ruby's house. They brought

30

boxes of toys and clothes with them, and an envelope of money. The things had come from people who wanted to help the family.

Lucielle told Dr. Broyard that Abon had lost his job. "Abon's good at a lot of things," she said. She wondered if there was work to be found at the NAACP.

Dr. Broyard didn't think so. "It may not be a good time for Abon to be looking. Better wait and let things simmer down."

The idea made Abon angry. "So I'm supposed to do nothing? Wait around and worry about how I'm gonna take care of my family?"

Dr. Broyard understood. "It's only temporary," he said. "In the meantime, the NAACP can provide for your family."

"And remember," Dr. Broyard's wife broke in, "what a privilege it is for Ruby to be doing this."

"A privilege?" Abon looked at Mrs. Broyard as if she were a little crazy. "Do any of those colored girls at the other school happen to be yours? Are any of them children of folks in the NAACP?"

Mrs. Broyard shook her head. Abon was just getting started. "How many of you people put *your* kids up for this *privilege*? How many of you had the *privilege* of losing your jobs?"

Chapter 12

"Fourteen, fifteen, sixteen . . . twenty!" Barbara Henry and Ruby were doing jumping jacks. The teacher stopped to catch her breath. And when she did, they could hear the mob yelling outside the school.

"Go home!" somebody shouted. "No niggers! Whites only!"

Barbara Henry sighed. She went over to shut the windows. "It'll be okay," she told Ruby.

"When are the other kids coming back?" Ruby asked. "When will this be like a normal school?"

Her teacher didn't know for sure. "They'll be back sometime," she said. "For now, you can think of this school as your very own. We can have fun, just the two of us, can't we?"

Ruby nodded. Mrs. Henry smiled at her. "It's lunchtime," the teacher announced. "I'll be back in thirty minutes."

Barbara greeted the men guarding the door, then headed for the teachers' lounge. She glanced into empty classrooms as she passed. The sound of a piano drew her toward the music room. One teacher was giving another a lesson.

Barbara stopped in the doorway. The woman playing the piano looked at her. "This lesson is private," she said. The other teacher closed the door in Barbara Henry's face.

It turned out to be a nice afternoon, perfect for a softball game. After school, everyone met at the lot on Logan Street. Ruby, her sister, Mary, and Alison were there. And Carl was there, too, getting in the way. He was little, but he wanted to play ball with his older sisters. Abon watched from the porch. He was smiling.

The smile faded as two cars pulled up in front of the house. The first was a fancy Cadillac that belonged to the Broyards. Abon hadn't seen the other car before, and he'd never seen the white people who climbed out of it.

Dr. Broyard introduced them, and Abon invited the new people inside. "Lucielle," he said, "this here's Dr. Coles and his wife. Dr. Coles is a psychiatrist."

"Call me Jane, please." Mrs. Coles held out her hand. Lucielle had been stringing popcorn for the Christmas tree. Before she took Jane's hand, Lucielle dusted hers on her apron.

Dr. Broyard glanced at his watch. He was in a hurry. "Sorry for just dropping by," he said, "but I thought you should meet Dr. Coles. I think Ruby will benefit from talking with him."

Abon frowned. "Ruby doesn't need no head-doctor," he said. "And, besides, we can't afford it."

33

"I wasn't planning to charge you," Bob Coles told him. "Listen, I've been watching Ruby. I've seen what she's going through. And I'd like to be of help."

When Abon refused, Bob Coles left his card on the kitchen table. He took Jane by the arm. They showed themselves out.

Strike one! Alison was up at bat. On third base, Ruby was trying to pay attention, but Carl kept getting in the way. "Go home," she told him. "Go home or I'll kill you, you little nigger!"

Carl started to cry. Mary stomped over to tell Ruby off. "I'm gonna tell Mama what you said."

Mary ran to the house. She was puffing a little. "Ruby called Carl a *nigger*!" she told her parents. "Ruby said she was gonna kill him."

Abon was stunned. He couldn't believe Ruby would say such a thing. But to Lucielle, Ruby's words made a horrible kind of sense. After all, Ruby had been hearing them every day.

Lucielle picked up the card Dr. Coles had left. She looked at it for a long time.

Chapter 13

"Can you draw me a picture of your school?" Dr. Coles asked Ruby. They were in the living room at Ruby's house. Dr. Coles passed her some crayons and paper. On the table beside them was a tape recorder. The recorder was on.

Ruby was happy to draw some pictures, which wasn't what Bob Coles had expected. "Tell me how you feel about your school."

"It's fun," Ruby said. "My teacher likes me." She drew some pink stick figures standing beside a building.

"Are these the people outside the school?" Bob Coles could hear the sound of laughter from the kitchen. His wife, Jane, was in there with Lucielle. "Is this how they look to you?"

Ruby looked at her picture. She had drawn the figures quickly, without much thought or detail. "I don't know how they look," Ruby told the doctor. "Because I don't really look at 'em."

"Why not, Ruby?" Coles thought he was on to something. "Why don't you look at the people?"

"My mama and the men told me not to," she said. As if that was that. Then Ruby changed the subject.

Jane Coles had fun. She told her husband about it as he drove them home. "They were lovely," she said. "Next time you should take time to just sit down and talk."

"I'm not there to be social," her husband snapped at her. "I'm trying to get some work done."

"What's wrong?" Jane asked, "Didn't things go well?"

"I don't get it," he told her. "Ruby says everything is fine at school, just fine. I don't understand it." When he stopped at a red light, Coles picked up some papers from the seat between them. He looked through the pictures Ruby had made.

"You'll figure it out," Jane said, but her husband wasn't listening. He was staring at a picture Ruby had drawn of her teacher and herself. She had used a pink crayon for both of them. Both were exactly the same color.

Ruby jolted awake in the middle of the night. Going to school had been terrible that morning. People were still yelling about killing her, threatening to poison her. And someone had held up a black doll in a coffin. Ruby had tried not to look, but she had seen it. And she had seen the coffin again in her dreams.

Ruby climbed out of bed and went to wake her mother. "You had a bad dream, baby?" her mother asked.

She rubbed her daughter's small shoulders. "Did you say your prayers?"

Ruby shook her head. "I didn't think so," Lucielle told her. "Now, go on back and get on your knees. Ask Jesus to take care of it."

And Ruby went back to kneel at the side of her bed. She prayed. She prayed as hard as she could.

Chapter 14

Ruby and Abon went together to Stein's grocery store. Something was wrong. Two people from the crowd were in there with Mrs. Stein. Mrs. Stein didn't say hello. When Ruby's father came up to the counter, Mrs. Stein asked him not to come to the store anymore.

Abon was surprised. "What?" he said. "Why?"

"Please," Mrs. Stein pleaded, "please just go."

Ruby's father was hurt. "Okay," he said, "if that's the way you want it. But just remember who was first to come in when you opened up, back when those rednecks wouldn't buy nothing from no Jews."

Mrs. Stein was trembling. She looked as if she might cry. Abon felt sorry for her, but he was still upset. "We never treated you no way but nice," he said. He took Ruby's hand and led her toward the door.

Now Ruby wasn't eating. She stared at the chicken on her plate, and thought about the people she had seen at Stein's. She thought about poison. When her mother asked what was wrong, Ruby said she wasn't hungry.

"Stop your foolishness," Lucielle told her. "You better clean that plate."

Ruby wouldn't. At last her mother got her to eat some chips and drink a cola. "What's wrong with my cooking," Lucielle scolded, "that you won't eat nothing but potato chips?"

"Does Mrs. Stein stand outside my school?" Ruby asked. "Does she say those bad things?"

Her mother was shocked by the very idea. "No," she said. "Mrs. Stein is Jewish. Those people at your school wouldn't be nice to her, either."

"Mrs. Stein said we couldn't come to her store again." Pain broke inside Ruby. "It's because of me, isn't it? How come no one likes me?"

"Oh, baby." Gently, Lucielle touched Ruby's face. "It's not you. It's just that you and those girls at the McDonogh School are doing something white people don't like. They don't want people of color mixed in with their children."

Her mother picked Ruby up and cuddled her in her lap. "No matter what those people say, you know God loves you. And you're so special and so smart, you deserve to go to any school you want."

Chapter 15

"*I'm gonna poison you 'til you choke to death!*" Ruby could hear the woman's scream rise above the mob. And then something else, the voice of one of the men, one of the marshals who was protecting her. "Get back," the marshal commanded. "I told you, sir! Get back!"

Ruby turned to see a man in a black suit coming toward her. She was terribly frightened. The marshal scooped her up in his arms and hurried into the school.

When the marshal let her down, Ruby ran to Barbara Henry. She clung to her and cried. Over Ruby's head, Barbara's eyes met the sad eyes of the marshal. He handed over Ruby's book bag, and the teacher led her away.

Outside, the man in the black suit was in trouble. He had been stopped by the men guarding Ruby. "I'm just trying to bring my daughter to school, sir," the man told them. He held his little girl's hand.

"Traitor!" the crowd yelled at the man. Someone spat at him. He was the first white parent to bring his child back to the William Frantz Public School. The girl was scared. She held on tightly to her daddy's hand.

The marshals stepped aside. The man in the black

suit and his child climbed the steep stairway into the building.

Ruby and Barbara Henry sat side by side at the teacher's desk. "You had a bad morning, didn't you?" Mrs. Henry asked Ruby softly.

Ruby didn't speak for a moment. Then she said, "I did all my homework, Mrs. Henry. Wanna see it?"

"In a minute," the teacher said. "Right now I want to talk about those people out there. They must have been raised with some funny ideas about people different from them."

The teacher looked down at Ruby's hands, and then she looked at her own. "See, they think that skin color is important. If your skin's not the same as theirs, they may not like you."

Ruby was fighting tears. Barbara Henry squeezed Ruby's hand. "Not all people are that way," she said. "Those people don't understand that everyone is special. Maybe one day they will."

"But why do they say those mean things to me?" A tear slipped down Ruby's cheek. "I didn't do nothing to them."

"No, honey, you didn't," the teacher said. "Those people are angry because the government is forcing them to do something they don't want to do. They feel kicked down."

Barbara touched Ruby's wet face. She felt like crying

herself. "When people feel kicked down," she said, "sometimes all they want to do is kick somebody else."

Alone at lunchtime, Ruby wouldn't touch her food. She hid her bologna sandwich in the closet of the classroom. She poured her milk into a jar of paste. If she didn't eat, she wouldn't choke. And she wouldn't have to worry about being poisoned.

Chapter 16

The guards at the barricade on Logan Street were getting used to Dr. Coles and his wife. They barely looked at the Ford. They just waved the car on through.

Bob Coles set up his tape recorder. He got out the crayons and paper. This time he thought he might draw pictures, too.

"A few came back last week," Ruby said. She got busy with her coloring. "Some kids came back to school, but none of 'em are in my class."

"Sounds like you're angry about that." Dr. Coles picked up a crayon. He was interested, but pretended that he wasn't. "And, you know, it's okay to say so. You're not a bad girl if you don't like something."

The sounds of talking came from the kitchen. And something smelled awfully good. From the half-open door, Abon looked in from time to time, checking on his daughter.

Ruby drew a picture of a pink girl with a big pink man. The little girl had a sad face. Dr. Coles looked at the picture. "Is that you, Ruby?"

"Nuh-uh," Ruby said. "That's my friend Alison and her daddy. Her daddy doesn't really like her to play with me anymore."

"Is Alison a white girl?" the doctor asked.

"No," Ruby told him, "she's like me."

Bob Coles was waiting for something like that. "I couldn't tell," he said. "Because you drew them with a pink crayon. And you color yourself pink, too." He held out a picture he had drawn. In his picture Ruby was brown.

Ruby made a face. "There's kindergartners who can draw better than that."

It was true. Coles looked at his picture and laughed. Ruby laughed along with him. From the doorway, Abon smiled. But he was worried about those drawings.

Jane was happy, excited. "Lucielle taught me to make red beans and rice," she told her husband. She tried to get him to sit down at the kitchen table. "It's a lot better than anything I've made before. You just have to try it!"

"We've got to go," Coles told her.

Jane was disappointed. Lucielle looked sorry, too. Lucielle said, "Well, at least let me give you a piece of pie to take with you."

"No," said Coles. "I'm not hungry. Thanks." The doctor wanted to get back to business. "Mr. and Mrs. Bridges," he said, "I'm a bit concerned about Ruby. Aside from the way she spoke to her brother, has she been behaving strangely?"

"No," Abon said. "Ruby's all right."

Lucielle was shaking her head. "Ruby doesn't eat like

she used to," she told Coles. "She's been turning up her nose at my good cooking. All she wants is packaged stuff like chips and cookies and Coke."

Bob Coles thought he knew why. But it was a hard thing to share. "There's a woman outside the school . . ." He looked down at the floor. "I apologize for having to say this. There's a woman who threatens to poison Ruby. She says she wants Ruby dead."

For a long while Abon sat and considered the picture of Jesus as a white man. Then he took it down from the wall and went upstairs to the bedroom. Lucielle was sitting on the edge of the bed. She was crying hard. "I thought we were doing the right thing," she sobbed. "How can they be so hateful to our little girl?"

Abon put the picture down and curled his arms around his wife. "Shhhh." He rocked her as if she were one of the children.

"I thought God wanted this to happen," she said. "I was trusting him. I've been praying. How can he let a little girl suffer?"

Abon stood up and put the picture of Jesus on the nightstand. "What do you think you're doing?" Lucielle asked.

"I was watching Ruby tonight. I was listening to her." Abon sighed. "She's got it in her head that white people are better than brown ones. She draws the colored folks all wrong and all the white folks perfect."

Lucielle didn't understand. "What's that got to do with Jesus?"

"Nobody knows what Jesus looked like," Abon said. "Seeing this picture tells Ruby that God looks like those people outside her school. It tells Ruby that God looks more like them than her."

Chapter 17

Jane was angry with her husband. When he asked if she was going to make dinner, she told him, "I already *had* a home-cooked meal at the Bridges'. And when you were offered the same, you *claimed* you weren't hungry." Jane turned her back to him and left the room.

Bob Coles spent a long time that night just staring up at the stars. He was thinking she was right. In the morning he said he was sorry. "I feel like a jerk, Jane."

"You should," she said. "You hurt Lucielle's feelings."

"Sorry," he said again. "I've been so focused on the work I'm supposed to be doing. There's a lot to find out about Ruby. She's so strong. And I don't know why. I've got to figure it out."

"Bob, why don't you try giving something?" Jane suggested. "Giving something of yourself?"

"What are you talking about?" he asked. "I'm helping her!"

"You're not helping Ruby," his wife replied. "You're studying her. And if you'd just stop being so professional and relate to her family as friends—"

He interrupted, "Which is going to accomplish what?"

"You want to know why she's so strong?" Jane was seeing something that he couldn't. "Did it ever occur to you that she might have gotten that strength from her parents?"

Abon was outside his house, cutting the grass. The lawn mower wasn't working so well. As the two sedans pulled up in front of the house, Abon gave the mower a good, hard slam. Ruby got out of the car. She ran toward him. "Daddy!" she yelled. "Daddy, I have to show you something."

He swooped her up into his arms, but she wiggled down again. Ruby took a paper from her book bag. Abon looked at it. "Arithmetic, A," he read aloud. "Spelling, A. Music, A. Art, A . . ."

"Straight A's!" Ruby was proud of herself.

"That's great, baby," he said. He smiled at her, but his smile was unhappy.

Ruby took a deep breath. "You lost your job 'cause of me," she said. "Didn't you, Daddy?"

Abon hugged her. "Don't you be worrying about me," he said. "I'm gonna be all right."

For a moment, Ruby looked as weighed down as her father. Then she drew herself up taller. "I've been praying to God to make you a new one," she said.

"Go on and play," Abon told her. "Mary and Carl are waiting for you. Now, go on."

* * *

Alison sat with Ruby at the bottom steps to Ruby's house, while the two friends played a game of Old Maid.

"Your daddy gonna let you be in the ball game next time we play?" Ruby asked her friend.

"Don't think so. Says colored folk ain't got time to be playing games," Alison said, looking down. "Says we gotta work hard if you wanna have something in this world."

Just then, Alison's father came out of her house. He was mad. "Alison! Where are you? You get in here," he demanded.

Mr. Lewis stomped up Logan Street while Alison began picking up her cards. She was nervous.

"I'm comin', Daddy," Alison shouted back.

Mr. Lewis was angry to see his daughter playing with Ruby. "What did I tell you?" he asked, just as he noticed Abon behind Ruby.

"Ain't no need to holler. I reckon we hear ya all right," Abon teased Mr. Lewis, which irritated him even more.

Mr. Lewis told Abon off. "Before your kid went to that school, this neighborhood was fine. Now we got barricades. We ain't welcome at Stein's. The white folks up the street are looking at us sideways. Now, colored folks are talkin' about boycotting Mardi Gras, which means my tavern ain't gonna do no business! So if I wanna holler, you sure are gonna hear me all right!"

Abon did not give Mr. Lewis the satisfaction of a response. Mr. Lewis grabbed Alison's hand and pulled her out of the yard. Ruby looked on, sad to see her friend leave and confused about why Alison could not stay. But she knew it was because of her.

Chapter 18

"*Traitor!*" A white woman led her two children through the screaming mob. The man in the black suit had already come and gone. "I'm gonna poison you!" the stocky woman shouted. Her son stood nearby. He had a look of longing in his eyes. He wanted to go back to school with his friends.

All at once, he broke away. He ran toward the building. "Jimmy!" his mother shouted. "Jimmy, you get back here!"

He turned to face his mother. His mind was made up. "I wanna go to school," he said. And Jimmy went up the staircase and into the building.

All alone, framed by the window of her classroom, Ruby watched.

"Now, you listen, Ruby," her mother said. "You were with me at the supermarket when I bought that food. You saw it was wrapped up tight. Nobody's put no poison in there. And I want you to eat it."

Ruby made a face, but she started eating. Lucielle was relieved. "Good girl," she said. She turned back to the stove and stirred a pot of red beans and rice.

"Mama?" Ruby asked. "You said those people outside my school would stop being so mean."

Lucielle put down the spoon. "They will, honey," she said. "They will."

Ruby looked at the food on her plate. She still wasn't feeling all that hungry. She asked her mother, "When?"

Her mother sat down beside her. She put her arm around Ruby. "You gotta put your trust in the Lord," she said. "Remember what I told you about Jesus praying for the very same people who hurt him?"

Ruby nodded. She remembered.

"Those mean people can't get to you," Lucielle told her daughter. "The men are there to protect you. And God loves you. He'll protect you, too."

Ruby's father came into the kitchen with Dr. and Mrs. Broyard. Dr. Broyard was carrying a box. "Hello there," he said. "I've got some goodies for you." Abon sighed. The big box reminded him that somebody else was providing for his family.

Mrs. Broyard sat down at the table. "Have you heard the latest?" she asked Lucielle. "People are talking about boycotting Mardi Gras this year!"

The box was filled with clothing. Ruby pressed a skirt against her waist. Too small. "You mean there won't be any parade?" she asked.

"We're asking colored people not to go to the festival, and not to be in the Mardi Gras parade," Dr. Broyard explained. "That will tell the city we're not happy about the way you and the girls at the McDonogh School have been treated."

Ruby was quiet, thinking that over. But when Mary snatched at the outfit Ruby was holding, Ruby gave her a push. Mary pushed back.

"Cut it out," their mother said, "or you'll both get spankings!" Lucielle looked over at Mrs. Broyard. "Y'all want to adopt some children?"

Mrs. Broyard smiled. "Actually, we'd love to have Ruby over for dinner sometime," she said. "We want to spend some time with her, you know, to help her feel supported."

"That would be nice," Lucielle told Mrs. Broyard. But Abon didn't agree. He left the room and went out to sit on the porch. He waited as the Broyards said their good-byes and drove off in their Cadillac.

Lucielle came out to join him. "I know you don't believe it," she said, "but I think they mean well. And it would be good for Ruby to see how they live. Show her what folks can have when they've got good educations."

Abon was disgusted. "Where are they when Ruby's having those nightmares? Or when Mary and Carl are getting teased 'cause I don't have a job?" He clenched his hands into fists. "The NAACP ain't here for any of that!"

With an effort, Abon tried to calm down. "Listen," he said. "They give us that stuff. They act like they're doing something nice. Because they know they're just using Ruby."

Chapter 19

Ruby waited by herself in the classroom. It was lunch-time and Mrs. Henry had gone off, as usual, to the teachers' lounge. From somewhere close, Ruby could hear the sound of laughter. There it was again, children's laughter!

Ruby went into the closet and peered through a key-hole. She could see five kids in the next room. They were giggling, skipping, having fun. Ruby watched them. She felt terribly alone.

When the teacher returned, Ruby wanted to talk about it. "I saw some of the other kids," she said. "How come they're all in a class together like in a normal school? How come I'm not?"

Mrs. Henry didn't know how to answer. After a moment, she asked, "Would you like to make some valentines?" She took out some red construction paper and picked up the jar of paste.

Something was wrong with the paste. It was much too thin. "Ugh," Barbara Henry said. "The humidity here is so awful."

Ruby just smiled at her teacher. She knew why the paste wouldn't work. It had to be all that milk.

Mrs. Barbara Henry went to talk with Miss Woodmere. "There's no good reason," she said, "that Ruby should be by herself. Especially as there are plenty of first graders who have returned to school."

Miss Woodmere's face held no hope for help, as usual. "Jill didn't want to teach that colored child, and nobody's going to force her."

"Fine," said Barbara. "Then let her kids come into Ruby's class and I'll teach them all together."

"No." Miss Woodmere shook her head.

Barbara Henry raised her voice. "This school was ordered to INTEGRATE! If you continue to keep Ruby separate, you are BREAKING federal law! Should we call the superintendent to discuss this? Or maybe President Kennedy?"

A red flush rose to Miss Woodmere's cheeks.

Not long after, Barbara led the kids from next door into Ruby's classroom. Ruby smiled at them, but they didn't know what to make of her. Mrs. Henry clapped her hands. "Let's play a game," she said. "You all know 'Duck, Duck, Goose.'"

The children sat in a circle, all except one. A girl went from one child to the next, tapping on their heads. "Duck." She tapped another girl. "Duck." She skipped Ruby's head and she tapped a little boy. "Duck."

Ruby grinned at the boy sitting next to her. It was

Jimmy. "My mommy told me not to play with you," he whispered. "Because you're a nigger." Ruby stopped smiling.

"Goose!" The girl tapped Jimmy on the head. But he didn't move at first. Then he got up and walked through the door and out into the hallway.

The little girl was confused. "Jimmy!" she called after him. "You're supposed to chase me! Jimmy!"

Chapter 20

"And how did that make you feel?" Dr. Coles asked Ruby. They were back in the living room. Ruby was coloring a picture.

"Jimmy didn't hurt my feelings," she said. "Not really. Because if my mama or daddy told me not to play with someone, it would be hard to go against that."

Ruby reached for another crayon. A blue one. "Alison's daddy told her not to play with me, either." Her voice sank to a whisper, "But she still does, sometimes."

Bob Coles whispered back. "I won't tell."

Ruby laughed. "Will *your* mama let you have some of my tea?" She pointed to her tea set and said in her best grown-up voice, "It's a special blend, imported from the North."

"Sure," he said. "I'll have some tea."

Ruby pretended to pour something into the teapot. "It won't take but a minute," she told him, "for the water to boil."

Dr. Coles was curious. "Would you be disappointed if my mommy told me not to have any tea with you?"

She looked at him with sudden sorrow. "I would be sad," she said. "Because you wouldn't visit me anymore. And we wouldn't be drawing pictures."

"Is it lonely in school?" he asked.

Ruby nodded. "When I'm by myself at lunchtime it is. And when the other kids are around. They don't want to play with me."

Tears came to Ruby's eyes, but she wiped them away. Bravely, she smiled at him. "Our tea is ready," she said. "We have to pray before we drink it."

The doctor watched as Ruby bowed her head. Bob Coles was learning more and more.

Ruby and Alison were playing jacks.

Ruby took a red necklace out of a bag of other things. The bag was full of paper confetti, and masks with sequins, and long strings of beads. They were left over from last year's Mardi Gras parade. Ruby looped some beads around her neck.

"What are you messing with that stuff for?" Alison asked. "Ain't nobody gonna go to Mardi Gras this time around. And that's your fault. Daddy says that's all because of *you*."

"I know that." Ruby took off the beads and put them slowly back into the bag.

Abon was listening to the girls. He was above them, up on a ladder, cleaning out the rain gutters. "Alison," he said. "Maybe you should run on home, before your daddy catches you playing. After all, you ain't got no time for that."

Alison picked up her jacks and walked away.

Mr. Taylor was coming up the sidewalk. His clothes were always splashed with bright color. He painted houses for a living. His wife was the one who sometimes helped with Ruby's hair. "Hey, Taylor," Abon called out to him. "How's it going?"

"Good," said Mr. Taylor. "Real good." He watched as Abon climbed down the ladder. "I wanted to ask you something," Mr. Taylor said. "I know the NAACP said it might not be time for you to be looking for work, but I surely could use your help."

Abon's face lit up. Before Taylor could say anything more, Abon was shaking his hand. Mr. Taylor said, "I can't pay you much, but it'll be something, anyway."

Ruby grinned at her father. "See, Daddy?" she said. She folded her hands together to remind him that he'd been in her prayers.

"Yes, baby," Abon said. "I see."

Chapter 21

The Broyards had paintings on the walls of their house, a chandelier, and a piano. They had two girls, both a few years older than Ruby. Ruby sat at their dining room table, trying to take it all in. "We used to have a picture of Jesus," she said. "But I think somebody stole it."

There was a lot of silverware next to her plate. Ruby picked out a fork. "How come y'all have so many pictures?"

Dr. Broyard glanced around. "We collect art," he said.

"How come?" Ruby asked.

One of the other girls giggled, but Dr. Broyard shushed her. "Art makes us feel good," he said. "Because of its great beauty."

Ruby wiped her fingertips on a napkin. It was made of cloth. "Here, honey pie," Mrs. Broyard whispered. "Place your napkin in your lap like this."

"Why?" Ruby wanted to know.

Mrs. Broyard smiled at her. "Because that's how little ladies use their napkins," she said. "Are you a little lady?"

Ruby nodded, but her attention had strayed to the piano in the living room. "After dinner," Mrs. Broyard promised, "I'll teach you your scales."

Ruby did very well at the piano. Mrs. Broyard taught her to play "Twinkle, Twinkle Little Star." Ruby was having a good time, but she wanted to ask about something. "Mrs. Broyard?" she said. "It's because of me that there's no Mardi Gras this year. Right?"

"It's because of you and those girls at the McDonogh School," Mrs. Broyard answered. "We're boycotting the carnival to show you our support."

Ruby was worried. "But won't everyone get mad about that? Won't they hate me then?"

"Oh, no," Mrs. Broyard told her. "People are staying home from the festival because they love you. They love what you're doing for them. They're staying home to show you that they care."

The next morning Ruby did something she'd never done before. As she passed through the mob, she stopped. She looked around at the people gathered outside her school.

Bob Coles saw her stop. He saw her lips move. He couldn't hear what Ruby was saying, but it made the crowd very angry. The shouting got so bad that finally one of the marshals swept Ruby up and carried her into the building.

Chapter 22

"But Ruby," Dr. Coles said. "I *saw* you talking to them. Were you telling them to leave you alone?" The tape recorder was on the kitchen table, picking up every word.

Ruby took another crayon. She drew a circle, then some eyes inside it. "I didn't tell them anything," she said. "I didn't talk to them."

"I was there!" Bob Coles told her. "I saw your lips moving!"

Ruby drew arms and stick-figure legs. "I wasn't talking to them. I was praying for them."

"Oh," the doctor said. "What was the prayer about?"

"I was asking God to help them understand," she said. "I said 'Please forgive these people here. Because even if they say bad things, they don't know what they're doing.'"

Ruby's picture was finished. "I'm going to hang my art on the wall," she said. "So we can see its beauty."

Ruby went out to the living room. Jane was there, helping Lucielle to feed the baby. The television was on. They were watching a story on the news. It was about Mardi Gras and the boycott.

Ruby kicked off her shoes and climbed on a chair. She

People surround the grassy lot on France Street, as they watch the softball game.

Ruby waves good-bye to her father as U.S. marshals drive her to William Frantz Public School.

Ruby and her mother are led through the crowd by U.S. marshals.

Dr. Robert Coles is impressed with Ruby's courage to walk through the angry crowd of protesters.

Mrs. Henry isn't afraid to be Ruby's teacher.

Ruby and her mother need the police escort even when they leave school.

Ruby bravely faces the mob without her mother.

Ruby's perseverance helped pave the way for desegregation in schools.

reached up to tape her drawing to the wall. "Do you always pray before school?" Bob Coles asked her.

Lucielle looked up from the TV screen. "Ruby prays in the car on her way there."

"But I forgot, Mama," Ruby said. "So I stopped and prayed out front."

Abon smiled at the doctor's reaction. "So how's my girl doing?" he asked.

"Fine," Coles told him. He thought about saying something else, but he couldn't put words to it. "Just fine."

"Dr. Coles?" Lucielle asked. "Would you like something to drink? Maybe some coffee or a cola?"

"Cola would be good," he told her. "And, please, call me Bob."

Ruby followed her mother back into the kitchen. Bob Coles turned to Abon. "So you want to know how she's doing?" he asked. "Just take a look at this drawing."

Abon looked at the picture on the wall. "She was coloring Negroes pink," he said. "She was coloring them all wrong."

Bob Coles laughed. "Look now," he said. "She's wearing that brown crayon out!"

Lucielle returned with a glass of cola and a small cup of gumbo. Coles tasted it. "Wow!" he said. "Oh, wow! This is really good."

When the doctor and his wife drove home that evening, Bob Coles couldn't stop talking about Ruby.

"I thought they were breaking her down," he said. "I thought they'd gotten to her and she was telling them off."

He came to a red light and stopped. "She was praying for them, Jane," he said. "She was blessing them."

Chapter 23

Ruby read a book aloud while the kids from Jill's class listened. All except Jimmy. He had his eyes closed and his fingers in his ears. He was missing the story.

Jill and Miss Woodmere were listening from the hallway. "She's a good teacher," Jill said. "My kids don't read that well yet."

Miss Woodmere frowned at Jill. She barged into the classroom, interrupting Ruby's reading. "Mrs. Henry," the vice principal announced, "there have been mice in this classroom. And I've brought the janitor to find out why."

Miss Woodmere and the janitor looked around the room. When Miss Woodmere opened the closet, her face took on a look of disgust. There was a pile of sandwiches in there, green and molding. Dozens of them.

Barbara Henry sat down beside Ruby. Ruby was nervous. "I'm not angry with you," Barbara said. "I'm just sorry you weren't eating your lunch."

"I've been eating," Ruby said. "More than I used to."

The teacher smiled at her. "Maybe lunchtime would be better if you had some company."

At twelve o'clock the teacher stayed. She didn't go to the lounge. She and her student ate together. Ruby ate her whole sandwich. And she drank her milk.

The next time Bob Coles went to Ruby's house he took a big box with him. Ruby was waiting for him. So were Mary and Carl. They each held up pictures to show to Dr. Coles. "See?" said Mary. "I draw good, too!"

Carl said, "Mine! Look at mine." He climbed into the doctor's lap and thrust a drawing under his nose.

The paper was awfully close to his eyes. Coles was *trying* to look at it, when Lucielle came in. "You two go on upstairs, now," she said.

As they turned to go, Coles smiled at them both. And they grinned back. "Those are good pictures," he said. "Really, really good."

When her brother and sister were safely gone, Ruby wanted to know about the box. "What's in there?" she asked.

It was a dollhouse, two stories high. It was beautiful. Ruby helped Coles set it up on the floor. "Let's play a game," he told her. "Let's pretend this is your school. These dolls are you and the other kids. Can you show me who they are and what they're like?"

Ruby picked up one of the dolls. It was a girl doll with a red dress. "This is Marie," Ruby told the doctor. "She's nice. And this one's Cathy. And this one is Carol. She's shy."

"Good," said Coles. "And these?"

"That one is Scott. This one can be Jimmy. Jimmy plays with me sometimes, but then he remembers he's not supposed to. And then he gets bad again."

"Does that make you angry?" Coles asked her. "Do you want to do bad things back?"

"Nuh-uh," Ruby said. "When you're bad, the bad will turn on you. Bad things always come back to you. If you're good, something good will happen. Do you want a cola?"

This time, Dr. Coles didn't mind that Ruby had changed the subject. He was thinking that she was pretty wonderful. "Sure," he said. And Ruby hopped up and went into the kitchen.

Abon caught the swinging door behind her. He leaned out to talk to Coles. "Cielle's teaching your wife to make that gumbo. And it's gonna be a while. When you're done here," Abon asked, "do you feel like taking a walk?"

The two men walked out into the warm evening. On their way down the sidewalk, they passed Mrs. Stein. She was going up to the house, carrying a box of groceries. She had come to say that she was sorry.

Abon felt better. "Things are finally calming down around here," he said with satisfaction.

Dr. Coles and Abon went into the corner bar. It was dark and smoky, and rich with the wail of blues music. Coles was the only white man there. "Did I tell you I got me a Purple Heart?" Abon asked him.

"Jane told me," Coles said. "How did you get it?"

"Got wounded in Korea. Saving a white soldier." Abon ordered a beer for himself and one for Bob Coles. "I never put much faith in integration," he said. "Even when we were fighting side by side, we were colored and they were white."

Abon took a sip of beer. "I risked my life for this country, got wounded for one of its own, and still we didn't really mix together." He gave Coles a look. "We sure never had no drinks together or nothing."

Self-consciously, Bob Coles smiled at him. He couldn't help asking, "Are you angry about all that?"

"Not really. Not anymore." Abon shook his head. "Anger wasn't doing me any good. I learned that from watching Ruby."

Coles laughed. "Oh," he said, "I believe it."

"Last time I got knocked down, Ruby showed me how to get back up." Abon looked into the mirror behind the counter. He could see his reflection, sitting next to that of Bob Coles. "Ruby's all faith, you know?"

Chapter 24

Barbara Henry held a booklet out to Ruby. "This is a test," she said, "to see how well you've done this year." She leaned down close and lowered her voice. "You take your time and do your best. I know you'll do well."

Ruby worked alone in the classroom. The windows were open to the coming springtime. Gradually, the crowd outside had thinned and gone home. There were only a few people there, too few for chants or shouting. All was quiet as Ruby filled out the answers.

Jill, the other first grade teacher, had warmed up to Ruby. During playtime with her class, the other children weren't exactly being friendly. When Ruby walked toward the piano, Jill followed her.

"Do you like music?" the teacher asked. "Would you like me to play something?"

Jill was surprised when Ruby sat down on the bench and played "Twinkle, Twinkle, Little Star."

One of the other girls in the class stood up and began to sing along with the piano. "Up above the world so high . . ." Ruby didn't falter. She kept playing. Her smile was bright and very happy.

When Barbara Henry came into Miss Woodmere's office, Miss Woodmere was smiling, which wasn't like her. "What can I do for you?" she asked.

"I came to see how Ruby scored on the test," the teacher said.

Miss Woodmere opened a filing cabinet. "I can tell you," she said. "I'm so glad this year is coming to a close. You haven't any idea." She took out a piece of paper from a file and handed it to Mrs. Henry.

"This is fabulous!" Barbara said. "These scores are incredible!"

"Exactly my thinking." Miss Woodmere's mouth drew tight. "Which is why I'm lowering them . . . to more accurately reflect a true assessment of Ruby's abilities."

Barbara Henry was stunned. "You can't do that!"

"I don't see why not," Miss Woodmere said. "Ruby has been privately tutored this year. She's had more attention paid to her than the other children."

"Is that what this is about?" Barbara's voice was rising. "You're upset because Ruby did better than the others?"

Miss Woodmere's face was remote. "Her score is too high, and I'll change it as I see fit."

"The score is accurate!" Barbara was yelling. "Ruby took the test all by herself. And the only reason she was privately taught is because YOU refused to mix her in with the other kids!"

"You tried to integrate that class." Miss Woodmere

pointed a finger. "You tried and you failed. Those children didn't accept Ruby at all."

"They *should* have accepted her," Barbara hissed. "It's only because their parents have taught them to hate." Barbara Henry stood up. She towered over Miss Woodmere. "You're a nasty woman," she said. "You're not going to get away with this! The country is changing, whether you like it or not."

The office workers and other teachers watched Barbara storm out of the room. Miss Woodmere went into her office without a word. Once her door closed, the women in the outer office couldn't contain themselves any longer. A few burst into laughter and others ran from the office to discuss what they had heard.

Chapter 25

The teachers' lounge was full of talk about the fight between Barbara Henry and the vice principal. The words had been heated and loud, and many people had overheard them. Because Jill had been in her classroom, one of the other teachers had to fill her in. "I heard the whole thing," she said. "Woodmere went and lowered Ruby's test score—"

Many of the teachers gathered their things together. They were ready to leave. Jill was not. She was furious. She stood up to face the vice principal. "Barbara Henry worked her behind off this year," she said. "She was dedicated to her job. And *your* job, Miss Woodmere, is to support your teachers. Not to *sabotage* them!"

The vice principal looked around the room. No one would meet her eyes. The other teachers agreed with Jill. Finally, Miss Woodmere just walked out, very much alone.

Barbara Henry had waited outside to tell Ruby good-bye. Together, they sat on the grass and read Ruby's favorite book. When Jill led her class to the playground, Ruby jumped up to join them. Barbara watched her walk over toward the merry-go-round. It was clear Ruby wanted to play.

"Barbara?" Jill wanted to say something. "I'm sorry we didn't become better friends this year. I believe you did the right thing. And I think you did it well. If I were as brave as you, I would have told you sooner."

Barbara Henry smiled at her. "That means a lot to me," she said. "And next year, if you get Ruby or someone like her in your class, you'll do the right thing, too."

Jill nodded. She would try. She looked away then, over at the kids in her class. They were going around and around, and Ruby was standing there watching. One of the little girls gestured for Ruby to get on.

Jimmy stopped the merry-go-round. He smiled at Ruby. She looked a little surprised, but she hopped right on. When the ride had picked up enough speed, Jimmy jumped up beside her. Ruby waved to Barbara. Barbara was elated and she waved back to Ruby. Tears welled up in her eyes. She was moved by Ruby's triumph *and* Jimmy's!

Chapter 26

When Jane and Bob Coles turned onto Ruby's street, there was something missing. There were no guards to wave them through. The barricades were gone. "That's a good sign," Jane told her husband.

A softball game was in progress on the grassy lot on Logan Street. Mary and Alison and Ruby were all playing. Sitting on the hood of a car, Abon was watching them. His clothes were splashed with paint. And he was looking happy.

Alison's daddy, Mr. Lewis, went over to sit beside him. "Ruby's playing real good these days," he said. "Have you been coaching her?"

"Ruby doesn't need my help," Abon told him. "She has *natural* talent."

"Yeah. Well, give yourself some credit." Mr. Lewis was a little uncomfortable. "She must have got some of it from you."

Abon looked at him. He saw the apology behind the words. "Whatever it is," Mr. Lewis continued, "we're proud of Ruby around here."

Bob Coles wasn't studying Ruby anymore. He was just visiting. He'd left the tape recorder at home, but he had

Make Sunday nights special
with The Wonderful
World of Disney

Your Favorite Films . . . Your Favorite Stars

Aladdin and the King of Thieves
Angels in the Endzone
Balloon Farm
Rodgers & Hammerstein's Cinderella
Flash
The Garbage Picking Field Goal
  Kicking Philadelphia Phenomenon
Goldrush: A Real Life Alaskan
  Adventure
Honey, We Shrunk Ourselves
Houseguest
Rudyard Kipling's Jungle Book
The Lion King
A Little Princess
Look Who's Talking Now
The Love Bug
Miracle at Midnight
Mr. Headmistress
My Date with the President's
  Daughter
Oliver Twist
Pocahontas
Principal Takes a Holiday
Ruby Bridges
Sabrina the Teenage Witch
Safety Patrol
The Santa Clause
Toothless
Tourist Trap
Tower of Terror

Whitney Houston
Whoopi Goldberg
Brandy
Richard Dreyfuss
Alyssa Milano
Christopher Lloyd
Kirstie Alley
Leslie Nielsen
Kirsten Dunst
Tony Danza
Tim Allen
Tom Hanks
Steve Guttenberg
Jason Alexander
Elijah Wood
and many more!

Watch every Sunday night on abc

You love the movies.
Now read the books.

Toy Story
The hilarious tale of toys that come to life, and a special friendship.

starring
Tom Hanks
Tim Allen

Tower of Terror
In 1939, five partygoers disappeared from a hotel elevator on their way up to the penthouse for a Halloween party. Can this chilling mystery be solved today by reenacting the fateful ride?

starring
Steve Guttenberg
Kirsten Dunst

Cinderella
The classic tale of romance and sibling rivalry retold with an all-star cast.

starring
Whitney Houston
Whoopi Goldberg
Brandy
Jason Alexander

Pocahontas
The story of a courageous young Native American woman who well understands the timeless value of living in harmony.

The Santa Clause
When Scott Calvin puts on Santa's red suit, his life is changed . . . forever.

starring
Tim Allen

The Love Bug
Herbie's back in an all-new adventure that includes his evil twin, "Horace, the Hate Bug"!

Ruby Bridges
The true story of six-year-old Ruby Bridges, one of the first African-American students to integrate public schools in New Orleans.

The Lion King
Join Simba, Nala, Timon, and Pumbaa as Simba battles his evil uncle Scar to become the king of the Pride Lands. .

The Wonderful World of Disney

At Bookstores Everywhere **Recapture the magic!**

© Disney

Epilogue

In 1994, Ruby Bridges-Hall established the Ruby Bridges Foundation, which seeks to improve conditions in New Orleans schools by encouraging parents to become more involved in their children's public school educations.

brought the crayons. Together, he and Ruby were drawing pictures and talking, just talking about things.

"I'm not gonna see Mrs. Henry for a while," Ruby told him. "No more school."

"I'm sure you'll see her again," the doctor said. "She's still your friend."

Ruby grinned at him. "Know what? I'm gonna have a birthday party real soon. And you and Mrs. Coles could come if you wanted to."

"Know what?" Coles returned. "We'll be there!" And Ruby cheered.

She held up a drawing for Bob Coles to see. It was a picture of her playing softball with Mary and Carl and the other kids in the neighborhood. The colors were right, and the faces she pictured were smiling.

There were some pink people mixed in with the brown. "This is you and Mrs. Coles," Ruby told him. "And that's Mrs. Henry."

"Why did you put us in with you?" Bob Coles asked.

"Because I wanted to," Ruby said. "I like you there." She pointed to a pink boy in the picture. "And that's Jimmy."

Bob Coles reached over and gave her a hug. But Ruby wasn't finished. "Jimmy is my friend now, even though his mama told him not to be," she said. "He doesn't act bad anymore. I think people are happier when they make friends. What do *you* think?"